the importance of being
being
you

by andrea stephens
and susie shellenberger

PUBLISHING
COLORADO SPRINGS, COLORADO

THE IMPORTANCE OF BEING YOU
Copyright © 1996 by Focus on the Family
All rights reserved. International copyright secured.

Library of Congress Cataloging-in-Publication Data
Stephens, Andrea.
　The importance of being you / by Andrea Stephens and Susie Shellenberger.
　　p. cm. — (Let's talk about life ; 2)
Summary: Discusses the concept of self-esteem for adolescent girls and offers practical suggestions to help them establish a healthy self-image.
　ISBN 1-56179-447-3
　1. Teenage girls—Religious life. 2. Teenage girls—Conduct of life. 3. Self-esteem in adolescence—Religious aspects—Christianity. 4. Christian life—Juvenile literature. [1. Self-esteem. 2. Christian life.] I. Shellenberger, Susie. II. Title. III. Series.
BV4551.2.S74　1996
248.8'33—dc20　　　　　　　　　　　　　　　　95-49797
　　　　　　　　　　　　　　　　　　　　　　　　CIP
　　　　　　　　　　　　　　　　　　　　　　　　AC

Published by Focus on the Family Publishing, Colorado Springs, Colorado 80995. Distributed in the U.S.A. and Canada by Word Books, Dallas, Texas.

Unless otherwise noted, Scripture taken from *The Living Bible*, copyright © 1971, owned by assignment by KNT Charitable Trust. All rights reserved.

No part of this publication may be reproduced, stored in a retrieval system, or transmitted in any form or by any means—electronic, mechanical, photocopy, recording, or otherwise—without prior permission of the publisher.

Cover design: The Puckett Group

Printed in the United States of America

97 98 99 00/10 9 8 7 6 5 4 3

Part One

Developing a Healthy Self-Image

~~~

What a terrific day! Sarah felt great. She'd aced the pop science quiz that Mrs. Hunter gave during third period, Brett said hi to her, and she actually finished all of her homework during study hall. Everything had gone super all day!

Leaving campus to go home, Sarah shifted the load of books she was carrying, and she suddenly lost her grip on them. They scattered all over the sidewalk just as a carload of guys drove by. One of them leaned out the window and shouted, "Klutz!" Sarah turned bright red with embarrassment.

Her best friend, walking behind her, saw what happened and caught up with her. "Way to go, clumsy," she teased. "You need a scholarship to charm school!"

That little incident planted a seed in Sarah's mind: *I'm a klutz. I'm stupid and clumsy, and I look silly.*

Like Sarah, most of us draw conclusions about who we are and what our value is by gathering information about ourselves from others. When a parent walks out on your family, when a boyfriend suddenly breaks up with you without an explanation, or when a close friend no longer speaks to you, your self-image is affected. Parents, brothers, sisters, friends, peers, teachers, coaches, employers, youth workers—all of these people play a part in the way you see yourself. How you interpret the statements they make about you, and the way they act and react toward you, will influence your self-image, or the mental picture you have of yourself.

What Is Self-Image?

Since we're talking about self-image, let's go ahead and define it—just to make sure we're all on the same track, okay?

The word *self* refers to YOU—the real person deep inside. *Image* means a mental picture. So, *self-image* is the picture, idea, or impression you have of yourself! Good or bad, everyone has a self-image. We could also use the term *self-concept*. They mean the same thing.

If you like yourself and focus on your good qualities, you have a positive self-image. If you don't like yourself very much and spend a lot of time thinking about the things you can't do well, you probably have a poor or negative self-image.

No one is born with a great self-image. Just like developing your personality or fine-tuning a skill, your self-worth is learned. It takes time to develop a healthy concept of yourself. Almost everyone struggles to establish a strong self-image during his or her teen years. You might be in the middle of the battle right now. If you don't like yourself, are you doomed to have a negative self-concept? No way!

Think of your school picture day. During the school year, everyone gets his or her class picture taken for the yearbook. On the day your class is scheduled to be photographed, you may or may *not* be feeling good about yourself. Maybe you woke up that morning with a small pimple on your face. And, as you file into the room where the pictures are being taken, you're saying to yourself, *I've got a zit the size of a volcano on my nose. What a terrible time for pictures!* But since this is the scheduled day for photos, you march in front of the camera right behind everyone else in your class.

A month later, when the pictures have been developed and your teacher is collecting the money, you have a choice to make. If you like the photos, you'll probably buy them. But if you're not satisfied, you can schedule another photo session on an upcoming day. In other words, you get another chance.

That's exactly the way it works with your self-concept. If you don't have a positive image of yourself right now, you can do something about it. You don't *have* to be stuck with a negative picture of yourself for the rest of your life.

How Is Self-Image Formed?

Many factors form your self-image. Some you have control over, others you don't. But again, the important thing to remember, as you discover the factors that have formed your self-concept, is that it IS *changeable!*

Sound complicated? It's really not. We'll walk through it together, okay? Go grab something to drink, and let's chat about the variety of things that contribute to establishing your self-image. You'll notice as we move along that negative factors always hinder a healthy self-concept. The good news, though, is that Christ offers a solution to every hardship we'll ever face. Okay, let's get going! We'll talk about the problems, and then we'll dive into the solutions.

Others' Comments

In our opening story, Sarah was feeling pretty good about herself until other people started making negative comments about her. Even though they were teasing, she took what they said to heart and her self-image plummeted. Many teens are like Sarah and base how they feel about themselves on what others say. Not only is this undependable, it's also dangerous! You're basing your mental picture of YOU on what others *say* about you. NEVER let others determine how you feel about yourself. Your self-image is too valuable.

How can you make sure you don't let others have this kind of negative influence over you? Here are some steps you can take.

1. Be selective. Before you accept what others say about you as *fact*, ask yourself these questions:

- Who is the person giving his or her opinion of me?
- Should I take this person's opinion seriously, or should I ignore it?
- What value or position does he or she hold in my life?
- Is this person a relative, an acquaintance, a casual friend, or a close friend?

Your relationship to the person will affect how seriously you take his or her opinion. A *close* friend's comments will count more than those of an acquaintance. But even friends tease a lot, and sometimes their comments need to be taken lightly. After all, they're in the middle of developing a self-image, too! Choosing friends who are honest, trustworthy, dependable, and most of all, caring Christians may minimize hurtful teasing.

2. Be forgiving. Like friends, parents tend to make comments about us that we take to heart. They drop hints or make direct statements that we take personally. They don't do this purposely to hurt our feelings. Most parents love their children very much and want what's best for us. Unfortunately, when they correct us in these ways, their *love* is not always the message we pick up.

Although we'd like to assume that everyone reading this book has loving folks, we have to be realistic and realize that some of you may be living with parents who are verbally abusive. We want you to know that God feels your hurt. Look at what the Bible says about Him in Psalm 34:18: "The Lord is close to those whose hearts are breaking."

One way God heals our hurt is to help us forgive those whose words have caused us pain. There are two main reasons He asks us to do this: (1) because *we've* been forgiven by Him and (2) so we'll once again be free to love those who have hurt us. God doesn't want us to be broken or to have broken relationships. Even though it might seem that the hurt will never go away, your heavenly Father can touch you with His healing power and make you whole. To heal you spiritually, emotionally, and physically is one of the reasons Jesus died for us. Ask Him to heal your hurt. It may be a process, but He'll do it!

3. Listen to your heavenly Father. If you want to develop a solid self-image, don't depend on others' opinions. That would be like building a house on quicksand. Instead, listen to what your heavenly Father says about you. After all, He created you in His image. Strive to tune *out* negative comments from those around you and tune *in* to His positive affirmation.

Check *this* out: "I have called you by name; you are mine" (Isaiah 43:1).

It feels good to have someone important call us by our names, doesn't it? It makes us feel special that an important person even *knows* our names. You're like an exquisite treasure to God. He paid a great price for your life. Is it any wonder that He loves you so much that He calls you by name?

But that's not all! Keep reading: "When you go through deep waters and great trouble, I will be with you. When you go through rivers of difficulty, you will not drown! When you walk through the fire of oppression, you will not be burned up—the flames will not consume you. For I am the Lord your God . . . " (Isaiah 43:2–3).

When those around you say unkind things, even in teasing, refuse to let that determine your self-worth. Jot down the above scriptures on a 3 x 5 card and carry it with you. Refer to it often, and let God's words influence how you feel about yourself.

Others' Expectations

Micki hated playing the piano, but she practiced every day after school and on Saturdays. Why? Because her mother wanted her to be a great pianist and Micki didn't want to disappoint her.

Susan knew that drinking alcohol, smoking cigarettes, and cutting classes were bad things to do, but she did them anyway. Why? Because she wanted the popular kids at her school to like her.

Trying to be who others expect you to be may make you act the way you think *they* want you to act. (Read that sentence one more time!) We all know people who try to be someone they're not. Why would anyone try to be what others think they should be? The answer to this question comes from a need that all of us have—to be loved and accepted. We want to feel that we're okay and approved of. Sometimes, like Susan, we'll even compromise what we believe, just to be accepted. Let's face it: Who wants to be a misfit or a social outcast? So, we try to please others by being what *they* want us to be.

But wait—is that really a good exchange? Doesn't that mean we're second best? Choosing to be what others want you to be might bring temporary acceptance, but it's not the real thing.

The real you is best. Why settle for second when you can be tops?

After God created the earth and everything in it, He looked around and said, "It is good." Guess what? Even though you weren't born yet, *you* were part of that creation. He expects great things from you. When He looks at you, He smiles and sees a life packed with all kinds of positive possibilities.

Throw your energy into meeting God's expectations of you rather than the expectations of your friends. What does God expect?

- He wants you to love those around you. (1 Corinthians 13)
- He desires that you depend on Him. (2 Corinthians 1:12)
- He yearns for you to become like Him. (Ephesians 4:15)
- He commands that you forgive those who have hurt you. (Ephesians 4:32)
- He calls you to tell others about Him. (Colossians 1:28)
- He expects you to live a holy life through the power of the Holy Spirit working through you. (Galatians 2:20)

God dreams BIG dreams for you. To help yourself consistently focus on that, memorize the proof: "Now glory be to God who by his mighty power at work within us is able to do far more than we would ever dare to ask or even dream of—infinitely beyond our highest prayers, desires, thoughts, or hopes" (Ephesians 3:20–21).

Others' Opinions

When I (Andrea) was a teenager, I had a strong desire to model. I got involved with fashion shows, learned how to apply makeup properly, and, like many other girls, daydreamed about having my picture on the cover of *Seventeen*. When I was a senior in high school, I sent a copy of my graduation picture to a top modeling agency. After several weeks, a response arrived.

The agency sent back my picture with the reply that I would never be a model and should look into another career. They didn't really explain why. I guess they're bombarded with so many photos of wannabes that they don't often take the time to share the reasons for their decisions.

But the agency executives *did* inform me that they were experts in the modeling field. I could seek the advice of others, they told me, but I would be wasting my time. I couldn't be a model.

Right then I had a decision to make. I could either believe what those "experts" said or stick with my inner feeling that I could be a model. I examined my motives, talked with people I trusted (parents, family members, Christian friends), and prayed . . . a lot.

In the end, I decided to hang in there. I

refused to let the opinion of the "experts"—people I didn't even know—determine how I felt about myself.

My determination paid off. Less than two years later, I was offered a modeling contract by Wilhelmina herself of Wilhelmina Models, Inc., and I moved to New York. I had several exciting national modeling jobs and the opportunity to meet many well-known people. I'm glad I decided not to accept the advice of the first agency.

Repeat after me: *When I let others' opinions of me form my self-image, it may limit me in fulfilling the desires of my heart.*

It doesn't matter what other people think. If *you* can see yourself fulfilling your secret dream, then you're well on your way to doing it. Why let others limit you? Besides, you have an unlimited God on your side! Remember . . . He dreams BIG dreams for you!

Your Experiences

Even though she had just turned 17, Jessica was given a lot of responsibility in her job as assistant manager of Kimby Toy Store. Every night she was supposed to count the money in the cash register, then leave $100 in the register and deposit the rest in the bank's night deposit box.

But one night she had a problem. She couldn't find the deposit box key. She usually kept it handy in her wallet, but it wasn't there.

She couldn't reach her manager, so Jessica decided the best thing was to take the money home. She would call her manager in the morning and explain where the money was. But she forgot to call.

At school the next day, during fourth period, Jessica was abruptly removed from class because of an emergency phone call. It was her manager at the toy store, and he was irate. Where was the money? How could she forget to call him? Why was she so irresponsible? Could she really be trusted?

Jessica was crushed. She had thought taking the money with her was the safest thing to do. She thought she was being responsible. The manager tried to make her feel lousy about herself. Of course, it was her fault she had not called him. But Jessica knew that, except for that oversight, she had acted in the best way.

You often draw conclusions about who you are from your own experiences. Sometimes these conclusions are right, and sometimes they're wrong. This depends on how you view the experience. Jessica could have decided she was careless and untrustworthy, but she didn't. Sure, she'd made a mistake, but that didn't make her a bad person.

There will always be times when you fail, disobey, or just plain mess up. As human beings, we *will* fall short of our own expectations, others' expectations of us, even God's expectations. Everyone has times when she fails a test, loses a game, misses an appointment, breaks a promise, snaps at her parents, or neglects her prayer time with the Lord. Some of these not-so-hot experiences are your own responsibility—like making the wrong decision when you know the right thing to do. Other experiences are caused by other people. These you have less control over.

You've probably heard the saying, "When life throws you lemons, make lemonade." That's pretty good advice! You *can* make the most of every experience you have. In other words, instead of allowing her boss to make her feel like a crook, Jessica *could* stop and think about how to make something positive come out of her situation. Sound impossible? Here are three ways to do it.

1. Be a detective. Stop and examine yourself. This will help you know when you need to make some positive changes. Even though Jessica's motive was right, she really shouldn't have taken the money. A better option would have been for her to leave a note for her employer. Or she could have asked her parents what to do. Maybe she should have stopped by the store early the next morning on her way to school.

If she's a good detective, she'll analyze the consequences of her actions, learn from them, and not make the same mistake again. The most important factor, though, is that she knows her own heart. Jessica knows her motive was right. So instead of allowing herself to think she's a jerk for making her boss assume she stole the money, she can feel good about herself for wanting to do the right thing.

2. *Forgive yourself.* Some people find it easier to forgive others than themselves. Try to teach yourself that failure is part of life. Learn to forgive yourself for your shortcomings. Easier said than done? The key is in striving to *forget* as well as *forgive*. Don't collect bad experiences. Give them to God, and let them go!

After Jessica apologized to her boss, she had a decision to make. Could she forgive herself for blowing it in her boss's eyes?

If you think you've forgiven yourself for something but continue to remind yourself of it, have you really forgiven yourself? Probably not!

God forgives you and forgets your sins when you sincerely ask Him. The Bible says He puts your sins as far as the east is from the west—and the east and west never meet! God isn't sitting in heaven with a scorecard of all your wrongs. He won't hold anything against you once you have asked His forgiveness. Do what Paul, a servant of Jesus, did. He said he forgot the past and looked toward the future.

If Jessica was going to do as God commands us, she would have to learn from her experience, put it in her past, and continue to do her job as a trusted employee.

3. Be a reflection of Christ. What would Christ do? He would forgive those who have hurt you! It's just as important that you do the same. This is tough, isn't it? In fact, it doesn't even seem fair. But the Lord tells us it's our *responsibility* to forgive.

Even though Jessica's feelings were hurt, she needed to forgive her boss for not trusting her. If she *didn't* forgive him, it would affect their relationship in a negative way and possibly even ruin it forever.

Successful experiences, failing experiences, good experiences, bad experiences . . . they all team up to help shape you into God's best!

Your Circumstances

The circumstances of your life also may affect the way you feel about yourself. Several years ago I (Andrea) attended a meeting at a counseling center for unwed teenage mothers. The goal of the center was to make it possible for girls to have their babies rather than let them think abortion was the only option. Toward the close of the meeting, a woman in her mid-twenties stood and walked to the front of the room. In a shy yet strong voice, she told us her story.

"My mother became pregnant as a teenager and was unmarried. She felt alone, embarrassed, and full of shame. She thought the only way out was to abort the tiny person growing inside her. But just before she was going to have the abortion, the Lord sent a woman into her life that she could trust and share her crisis with. This special woman made it possible for my mother to do what she really wanted—give birth to her baby. That baby was me."

The young woman standing before us did not choose to be born into a situation that gave her no family, no sense of belonging, and years of wondering why her real father didn't want her. These were circumstances in her life over which she had no control. And they were unchangeable. But she was given the greatest gift: life.

You can choose to accept or reject the circumstances in your life that are unchangeable. Your parents, your brothers and sisters, your birth position in your family, your race, your skin color, and the fact that you are a female—all of these are circumstances you were born into, and you can't change them. Whether or not you accept these circumstances will affect your self-image.

Realizing that each of your unchangeable circumstances has been given to you for a purpose will help you begin to accept them. Your life—all it is and all it isn't—is God's gift to you; what you do with it is *your* gift to God. Like the young woman we just met, see how you can take what you have been given and make something good out of it. Let your circumstances help build up your self-image rather than get you down.

Your Physical Appearance

Another thing that influences your self-image is your physical appearance. If you're like most people, you have some physical features you'd be much happier without—things you'd trade in with no hesitation. Oh, if only that were possible!

We live in a society that says if you don't like your appearance, change it! Nose too long? Get it shortened. Eyes not green enough? Colored contacts will fix that. Hair won't curl? Perm it. Hair won't lie flat? Straighten it. Don't want brown hair? Become a blonde—directly from a bottle. Not happy with your bust line? Two thousand dollars will get you a new one. Nails refuse to grow? Slap on some acrylic ones. The list goes on and on.

Why do so many women today, young and old, have such a hard time accepting their God-given appearance? There are many reasons, but let's focus on the four biggest ones.

They Don't Fit Society's Standard of Beauty

American culture is obsessed with physical beauty. Every billboard and magazine cover sends us the same message. Surely you need an oval face, high cheekbones, perfectly straight white teeth, bouncing hair, flawless skin, and weigh not an ounce over 110 pounds to be accepted. Right? WRONG! Less than 1 percent of the world's population has these combined characteristics. And here's news. Almost every picture-perfect face you see in print has been airbrushed to look flawless! Even Cindy Crawford says that it takes an entire crew of people several hours to give her the "unmade-up, just woke up" look.

Whether it's removing pimples, whitening teeth, or even concealing some freckles, magazine-cover models have ALL been touched up and meticulously worked on to appear perfect. But guess what? Madison Avenue is not promoting reality. It's selling a fantasy.

It's difficult to escape the pressure of trying to look like a cover girl in order to gain self-acceptance and the attention of others. Women, and especially teens, end up believing in these beauty standards that really are *impossible* to achieve. Then, when we compare our own appearance with these standards, what happens? We don't measure up. But how could we? We're comparing ourselves against a false image. Yet we feel like going through life with paper bags over our heads!

It's our guess that none of you had a thing to do with the way you look. While you were still inside your mother, did she call you up on the umbilical cord to ask what you wanted to look like? Did anyone let you put in special requests before you were designed? We know *we* didn't get that chance. We would have asked for a few changes!

They're Teased About Their Looks

The second reason most girls have such a tough time accepting their physical appearance is they've been teased about their looks. This teasing begins when we're children. "Where did you get all those freckles?" "My goodness, you're a skinny little thing. Don't you ever eat?" Or, "I'll bet your mother never has leftovers at your house." People can be thoughtless when it comes to identifying your differences. Of course, they always pick a feature you can't help! Big noses are referred to as ski slopes, and oversized ears are often called Dumbo ears. What about Bozo Hair, Four Eyes, and Metal Mouth? Any of these sound familiar? I (Andrea) was continually called Bird Legs as a kid. So my legs were skinny. No fault of mine!

Nicknames are often unfair. They can hurt us more than people realize. We call them "kicknames" because that's exactly what they do! These seemingly playful put-downs, when connected to your physical appearance, can make you question your looks.

Please don't take someone's sorry sense of

humor to heart! People who tease and put others down are usually struggling with their own self-acceptance. Sometimes they actually think their comments are cute, but they're interpreted by you as faultfinding.

Ephesians 4:29 says that we are to edify one another. *Edify* means "to build up." We are to build each other up, not put each other down. Do you build up or put down those around you? And what about yourself? This principle applies to the things you say to *yourself* as well. Stop insulting yourself and others. You are a precious person. Build yourself and others up in the Lord.

They Aren't Popular

Not getting enough attention may be another reason behind not liking your appearance. Some kids feel the whole world is ignoring them, so they must be ugly! Ever sit home on a Saturday night without a date, convincing yourself that you're not as cute as Samantha Smoozy, who always has a date? Not getting the attention you need or want may have *nothing* to do with your looks. However, the effect will be the same if you think it does.

Look at the girl who gets attention *only* because she looks great. Maybe no one takes her seriously as a person. Perhaps she's just good to look at and makes the guys who go with her look good. (Remember, guys have self-image problems, too.)

Being liked for who you are on the inside is far more important. As Christians we have an extra bonus when it comes to attention. We have a Lord who is always available to give us His love and to focus completely on us. We matter to Him. He cares how we feel.

They're Struggling to Accept the Changes of Womanhood

Try to remember that during your preteen and teen years, your body (and the body of every girl in the whole world) is going through a tremendous amount of change. Change means adjustment, and adjustment isn't always easy.

Your body is in the process of changing from a little girl to a young lady. Your breasts are beginning to develop, and they may not even be the same size yet. That's okay. You're normal! (They don't grow at the same time or the same rate, but they'll eventually even out.)

You're also beginning your menstrual cycle, and that can even be frightening at times. You may be fearful of starting your period while you're at school or church. (Let us encourage you to pick up the first book in our Let's Talk About Life series. It discusses in detail the menstrual cycle, tampons, pads, and several other things that are happening inside your body.)

You'll begin to gain weight, grow pubic

hair, and maybe even shoot up a few inches. But on top of all the *physical* changes, you'll also experience *physiological* changes. It's as if your hormones suddenly wake up and start screaming. Your moods will often shift from being happy and excited to sad and lonely. One evening while your family is watching TV, you might crawl into your mom's lap or snuggle close to your dad, and the very next day you'll feel desperate for independence. What's going on? Again, you're normal, and you're becoming a woman.

If you focus on your changing body, it can affect your self-concept. Try to accept the fact that a changing body will sometimes feel weird. But strive not to let that affect how you feel about yourself as a person. In a few years, you'll look back on this time of bodily changes and probably think, *I guess it wasn't THAT bad!*

Your Limitations, Real or Imagined

There are really only a few things that might limit you in doing and becoming all you wish. Let's discuss a few.

Physical Limitations

If you're four feet, eight inches tall, you probably won't be a star basketball player. If you have poor eyesight, you'll never be a commercial pilot. If you're six feet tall, you probably won't be a jockey.

In other words, try to be realistic when assessing your ability to accomplish a specific dream. It may simply be physically impossible for you to achieve a particular goal. Does that mean we should throw in the towel and assume we can't do *anything*? No. But it *could* mean we need to alter our vision. If it's not physically possible for you to be a star basketball player, consider devoting your time to keeping the stat sheets for the basketball team. If that doesn't interest you, think about trying out for the track team.

As a teenager, Joni Eareckson Tada loved riding horses. She may even have dreamed of riding professionally. But in her teen years, she was injured in a diving accident and left confined to a wheelchair as a quadriplegic. She could have chosen to wallow in self-pity and a negative self-concept. But she chose, instead, to allow God to give her a *new* vision.

Through many trials and tears, Joni developed some incredible talents. She learned to draw by holding a pencil in her mouth and is now well known for her artwork. She didn't stop there, though. Joni began to write and is now a respected author. Time to quit? Not hardly! Joni also developed her voice and has released several music albums.

With God's help, it *is* possible to make the most of your life. Because of physical limitations, you may need to shift some of your dreams, but God will do mighty things in the lives of His willing children.

Lack of Knowledge

Many people do not attempt to do things they feel ignorant about. I (Andrea) can't speak Spanish, but that's because I've never been taught. It's not a matter of being stupid or limited; it's because I've never taken the time to learn. The Bible tells us in Proverbs 10:14 that people who are wise store up or grow in knowledge. Learning is very important. Some kids don't like school (or at least don't take it seriously). We hope you're wise enough to know how valuable a good education is. You don't have to let lack of knowledge limit you.

Self-Doubt

If you think you can't, you won't. Believe in your heart you can do it! Why? Because from your heart you will get the strength to complete the task that is facing you. Many times in Scripture we are encouraged to be *believers*, not doubters. Jesus referred to His disciples as men of little faith. He wants *us* to be disciples of BIG faith. One of the apostles, Thomas, better known as "Doubting Thomas," was told by Jesus: "Don't be faithless any longer. Believe!" (John 20:27). We need to understand that what the angel told Mary, the mother of Jesus, is true: "Nothing will be impossible with God" (Luke 1:37, New American Standard). Believing in God's plan for you is the key to overcoming doubt.

15 PRACTICAL WAYS TO DEVELOP A HEALTHY SELF-IMAGE

We've looked at some major influences in the development of your self-image: people, experiences, circumstances, physical appearance, and real or imagined limitations. Therefore, you have already learned a few ways to improve your self-image. First, evaluate the things others are saying before you accept them as fact. Second, learn from unsuccessful experiences and be forgiving toward yourself and others. Third, accept the circumstances in your life that you can't change. Fourth, learn to love God's design for your physical appearance. And finally, believe in yourself! Each of these will give you a good start on improving your self-image.

Still need an image booster? Try these 15 tips!

1. Remember that God designed you.
Maybe you struggle with your looks because you don't truly understand who your designer is. When God created the first man and woman, He said, "It is very good." YOU are a special part of His creation. He's extremely capable of bringing out your best—emphasizing your uniqueness.

Everything God creates is beautiful and has value. The Lord wants you to know in your heart that He has placed His stamp of approval on you.

You are much more than just a little bit of your mother and father mixed together. Your parents had a lot to do with your appearance, but God knew who you would be long before you were born. In fact, you were His idea!

In Genesis, the first book of the Bible, God says that He made us in His image and likeness. Of all the creatures He created, God chose *us* to be like Him. What an honor!

The Bible says God's hands fashioned you and made you. You're *handmade!* Psalm 139:13–14 says that God formed your inward parts and wove you while you were still growing inside your mother. Look closely at a weaving and you'll notice each strand of yarn is placed carefully to create the design the artist wanted. This is the same kind of care and planning God used to make you.

The passage goes on to say that you are fearfully and wonderfully made. The word *fearfully* means with honor and respect, not that God was afraid when He made you. Verse 15 says that your frame—your bone structure—is uniquely yours. You must be pretty important.

Most amazing of all, the Bible tells you in Genesis 2:7 that it is God's very breath that gave life to Adam, the first human being. That creation cycle continues today. God's breath has given *you* life.

Wow! You *are* God-created. Is there any question left in your mind? You are a unique creation, handcrafted by the Master Designer. There's no stamp on you that says MADE IN AMERICA. It says MADE IN HEAVEN! The Lord made you beautiful, and He loves how He made you. He sees you through eyes of love. He sees you as you really are.

You can develop a healthy self-image by accepting God's design for you. Which will you choose to believe—the world's beauty standards or God's?

2. See yourself as one-of-a-kind. "But wait," you say. "What about the things *I* don't like about my appearance? What about the physical marks and shapes I think are mistakes?" Here's the answer: These things are far from flaws; they are the intricate details of your individual appearance that make you *one-of-a-kind*. There is no one else like you. No one can take your place. We're so glad God didn't have just one or two "people" molds. If we all looked and acted alike, life would be much less exciting!

The details of your appearance do not make you different in a negative sense. They make you special. You have a certain look that sets you apart from all others. Accepting this will help you achieve God's purpose for your life.

"But I'm not just talking about physical stuff," you say. "What about my personality flaws?" Well, now *that's* something you *can* work on!

If you're short-tempered, ask your parents or youth leader to help you improve. They can hold you accountable in a loving way. Perhaps you're impatient. Again, this is something you can work on. Too sarcastic? Make a conscious effort to be kinder.

3. Take care of yourself. Let's talk straight, okay? Those who mess around with drugs, alcohol, or cigarettes usually have low self-esteem. They feel lousy about themselves, and they think that drinking, smoking, or taking drugs will either make them feel better or help them temporarily forget how much they hate themselves.

Don't fall into that trap! Your body is God's wonderful creation. Treat it as a precious jewel. Guard it carefully. Get the proper amount of sleep you need to be at your best in school or church, and strive to eat a balanced diet. Plan regular times to exercise and tone your body. You won't regret it!

4. Avoid the comparison game. Beware! Don't compare yourself with others, especially in specific areas you can't change. Comparing only leads to one of two conclusions: (1) You're better than so-and-so, or (2) you're not as good as so-and-so. Both of these attitudes are wrong. The first one is prideful and conceited. The second one makes you feel inferior—as if you don't measure up. You'll often meet people you think are more attractive than you, and you'll meet others you think are less attractive. Remembering that *in God's eyes all of us are equally beautiful* will help you not to compare.

5. Develop a good snapshot. Get a good mental picture of the new image you want, and grow into it. Remember that self-image is the picture, idea, or impression you have of yourself. Again, strive to use God's picture of yourself as your example.

God loves you just the way He designed you! And He wants *you* to love you also! He wants you to see yourself as the valuable young woman He's created you to be—loving, believing in, and being yourself. A good self-image is the first priority in developing a more beautiful you. That's what this book is about: first, to accept yourself as you are, even though you think you are not the "ideal"; and second, to discover how to take what you are and enhance it so that you make the most of what God has given you. Now, *that's* a good snapshot!

6. Set goals. Include several short-term goals you can reach quickly and with some ease. This will build your success rate and make you feel like you're getting somewhere. This is a real confidence builder.

Do you have a goal of running for class office, yet you never know what to say when you're with people? How about asking your Sunday school teacher or pastor if you can tag along when he or she visits people? You wouldn't have to say anything until you're comfortable, but you'd be able to watch and learn from what *he or she* does.

As your confidence grows, begin talking to the people you visit. If you call on an elderly lady, you might ask her to share a favorite memory with you. In time, you'll begin to feel confident about talking to those around you.

Do you have some goals that seem impossible? That's okay. Remember: You serve a BIG God who wants to help you meet your goals!

7. Be you! The ultimate result of a low self-image is total dislike of yourself—the belief that you have no value and nothing to contribute to life, that everything you do is wrong. *Oh,* you think, *if only I could be someone else!*

Almost every teen we know struggles, at some point in time, with a low self-image. They feel as if they just don't measure up and aren't as good as others.

Is there a way to overcome it? Yes! In fact, we've already hinted at it. Discover who you are and how you fit into your Creator's plan. To understand how uniquely you have been created, to discover the gifts and talents you have, and to accept the fact that God loves you will help you become excited about being unique.

Your self-image can be your worst enemy or your best friend. It will either limit you or allow you to grow. How you see yourself, how you think others see you, and the way you feel about yourself affect almost every area of your life.

8. Be an explorer. Discover your gifts and talents. What do you enjoy doing? What are you skilled at? Sports, music, working with children, art—the list goes on. You might have the ability to make others feel at ease around you. That's a special trait! Or you may have the gift of hospitality—you might enjoy planning a full evening and having friends over to your house. Don't take these special gifts for granted. Use them! As you become more confident in the things you do well, you'll desire to try your hand at a variety of other things you're interested in.

9. List your attributes. Jot down 25 good things about yourself. You may have to think hard, but you can do it! Do you have straight teeth? Others would die for great teeth! Write it down. Do you have nice handwriting? Put it on the list. What about your consistency? Do you finish most projects you start? Add it to your list.

If you also discover some not-so-hot things about yourself, such as character traits that you can improve, write them down also, and see how you can change them so that you can add them to your good attributes list. For example, if you tend to be stingy with your possessions, work on yourself until the stinginess is transformed into generosity.

10. Pick your pals carefully. Surround yourself with honest and dependable Christian friends, those who make you feel good about who you are. If your closest friends are people who share your values and morals, you'll be less tempted to do things you shouldn't. Whenever you get into the habit of doing things behind your parents' backs, it causes you to feel bad about yourself. And guess what? THAT results in a negative self-concept.

Be kind to *everyone*, but be extremely selective with whom you choose to become intimate friends. By choosing pals who share your standards, you'll be investing in positive friendships. And—you guessed it—affirming friends help establish a positive self-image.

11. Stretch your mind. Learn a new subject or hobby. Expand yourself. Set aside some special time each week (maybe every Saturday) to practice something you've always wanted to learn. Have you ever wanted to ride a unicycle? Now's the time to do it! Or what about calligraphy? You could make your own Christmas cards with elegant messages next holiday season. Or how about cake decorating? You could be in big demand for birthday parties and special events. Perhaps you've always wanted to learn a foreign language that's not offered in your junior high or high school. Ask your parents if they'd consider allowing you to study it at a local college or university. The possibilities are endless! And the more things you realize you're good at, the more you're enhancing your self-worth.

12. *Read the Bible and pray daily.* You can always find a message of love and hope in the Bible. The more you read, the more you will realize you can do *all* things with Jesus.

By developing a stronger relationship with God, you'll notice that His opinions and standards will soon outweigh those of the world. Try to saturate yourself with Scripture. Choose key verses to memorize. If memorization is hard for you, ask a friend to join you in this venture. Encourage each other by rewarding yourselves when you've each learned five verses. You'll soon realize the powerful difference God's view—instead of the world's—will make in your life.

13. *Initiate some random acts of kindness.* Try some quick picker-uppers. Do something special for yourself or for someone else. This will work wonders for liking yourself better.

- Wear a new hairstyle or outfit.
- Place a fresh-cut flower in a vase on someone's bedside table.
- Take a nice long bubble bath.

- Buy some treats for the neighbor's dog.
- Clean the house without being asked.
- Get a manicure.
- Go to a grocery store and help carry an elderly person's groceries.
- Bake a dessert you've never made before.
- Write an encouraging note to five people you appreciate.

Now it's *your* turn. List three other random acts of kindness you can do for yourself or for someone else.

-
-
-

14. Believe in yourself. God has begun a good thing in you, and He *will* complete it. Jot this down on a 3 x 5 card: "I am a STAR of God's creation! I believe in (write your name). Lord, teach me that You love me today."

By saying you're a star of God's creation, you're telling God that you realize what He created is very, very good. By asking Him to teach you that He loves you, you're forming a mind-set that will be on the lookout for positive signs of His love throughout the day. You'll be surprised at the fun difference it will make in how you feel about yourself!

15. Be realistic. Realize that there will be times when you'll be in a slump. When that happens, pray and seek out close Christian friends and family members who can remind you of your worth.

Even adults suffer from poor self-image from time to time. It's normal to experience times of doubting yourself. But just because everyone goes through this doesn't mean you have to stay there! Read the following verses out loud when you're down in the dumps, and trust Christ to set you back on a positive course.

"We are pressed on every side by troubles, but not crushed and broken. We are perplexed because we don't know why things happen as they do, but we don't give up and quit. We are hunted down, but God never abandons us. We get knocked down, but we get up again and keep going" (2 Corinthians 4:8–9).

"Fear not, for I am with you. Do not be dismayed. I am your God. I will strengthen you; I will help you; I will uphold you with my victorious right hand" (Isaiah 41:10).

"O my soul, why be so gloomy and discouraged? Trust in God! I shall again praise him for his wondrous help; he will make me smile again, *for he is my God!*" (Psalm 43:5).

Having a healthy, clear image of who you are is truly the beginning of a beautiful you. Beauty begins on the inside, then shines outward.

Part Two

Developing Your Inner Beauty

~~~

When I (Andrea) was younger, I was totally obsessed with beauty. I stared at magazine covers and gorgeous makeup and hair advertisements all the time. Beautiful-looking people really had it all together. They had the upper hand in life. At least that's what *I* thought.

It was when I was modeling in New York City that God opened my eyes to see the true definition of the word *beauty*. Actually, the whole lesson centered around another model named Janice. Here's what happened.

Those of us who were new models spent most of our time taking test pictures, hoping to put together a dynamic portfolio. That's when I met Janice. She had been with the agency a little longer than I, and she was beautiful—you know, one of those girls many others wished they looked like.

Well, one afternoon after I had been test shooting, I stopped in at the agency. The room buzzed with ringing telephones, busy bookers, and a few models, one of whom was Janice. The attention was centered on her. Everyone seemed to be in awe of Janice's sudden weight loss. I listened to her explanation of how "it was nothing." She had just taken up jogging and quit eating so much. "After all," she exclaimed, "what is there worth eating anyway?"

Are you kidding? I *loved* the variety of food New York had to offer. Every corner had a vendor selling some sort of tempting treat. Trail mix, roasted cashews, hot dogs, and pizza by the slice.

As I sat there listening, the subject changed to Janice's new boyfriend and how good-looking he was. Janice's language became crude, and I began to feel uncomfortable.

Off to her next appointment, she strutted out of the room. That's when the truth about her weight loss was uncovered. "Want to know what I heard about Janice's 'Oh, it was nothing' weight loss?" one of the models said. "Janice didn't sweat one drop to lose a pound. She just popped pills." She paused. "Speed." A hush came over the room. Drugs? And *I* had thought she had it all. Janice looked fantastic on the outside, but inside she struggled greatly.

I suddenly began to feel sorry for her. Here was a young lady with tons of potential who was destroying herself emotionally, physically, and spiritually. She was so driven to be a top model that she resorted to using drugs to help her attain it.

I learned a lesson that day: Outer beauty simply isn't worth what the world says it is. The *real* treasure is inner beauty—loving yourself for who God made you to be, and learning to accept your strengths *as well as* your weaknesses. THAT'S model material. And that's exactly the kind of beauty *I* want.

WHAT IS INNER BEAUTY?

When we ask girls what their definition of *inner* beauty is, many tell us they think of someone who is kind, unselfish, and loving toward others. Maybe you would say, "A person with inner beauty is one who is at peace with herself, goes to church, and is nice to kids at school—even to the ones no one else likes."

Well, all of these definitions are correct. They each describe loving and thoughtful actions rather than appearance. Inner beauty is not based on what you *look* like, but what you *act* like.

Think about the important people in your life. Are they special because of their appearance? No. It's probably because of their kindness, loyalty, friendship, or maybe because they are always there when you need them. It's because of their inner beauty.

Jesus was like that. People liked Him not because He was "tall, dark, and handsome." Listen to how the prophet Isaiah described Jesus: "But in our eyes there was no attractiveness at all, nothing to make us want him" (Isaiah 53:2).

What was it, then, that caused people to be drawn to Him by the thousands? What made Jesus so magnetic? It was because of the person He was on the inside. It was His *inner* beauty.

Jesus was kind to the poor woman at the well and traveled miles to lay hands on people who were sick. He came along at just the right moment to assist fishermen with their catch for the day. He made time in His busy schedule to eat a meal with those who needed His forgiveness and His company. And, oh, how He served! He provided food for thousands, and He lovingly washed the sweaty, dirty feet of the disciples. His giving showed that He cared. Ultimately, He gave everything . . . even His *life!*

It wasn't Jesus' appearance that made Him beautiful. It was His heart. What's in a person's heart will affect the amount of inner beauty he or she has. What's in our hearts usually determines our actions. Do you have a heart filled with love or hatefulness? Forgiveness or resentment? Caring or indifference? Joyfulness or depression?

The Lord is keeping watch over our hearts. Check out 1 Samuel 16:7: "But the Lord said to Samuel, 'Don't judge by a man's face or height.... I don't make decisions the way you do! Men judge by outward appearance, but I look at a man's thoughts and intentions.'"

It's true that we notice the outer appearance of others first. Then as we get to know them, we begin to see their inner appearance—their hearts. That's where God looks. He really wants us to be beautiful on the inside. He wants us to act in loving ways—to reflect His love and His image. He wants our hearts to be filled with *consideration*, *contentment*, and *consistency*. These are three key building blocks to inner beauty.

Consideration

Katie had worked earnestly in anticipation of this day—cheerleading tryouts. Her older sister had even practiced with her, teaching her fancy footsteps, routines, high kicks, and enthusiastic smiles. Katie had mastered them all in hopes of winning the judges' favor. She was confident and felt good about what she'd learned.

When Katie arrived early at the gym, she drew a number to see where she would fall in the tryout order. Number two! This would give her a chance to perform for the judges before almost all of the other girls. It meant everything to Katie to make it as a cheerleader, and being number two was more than she could have asked.

The other girls arrived. Some were excited, some were scared, but most of them were quietly rehearsing their routines.

Katie looked at her watch. Only a few more minutes, and her big moment would be here.

Glancing around, she noticed Heather, a friend from English class, standing away from the others. Heather looked frantic! She was pacing rapidly back and forth and wringing her hands. Katie made her way through swinging arms and kicking legs to her friend.

"Hi, Heather," Katie said.

"Oh. Hi, Katie." Heather didn't look up as she paced.

"Everyone's practicing like crazy," Katie said. "Do you want to rehearse? I mean, if you need to work on a cheer, I could help you real quick." Katie rushed the words out, knowing tryouts were about to start.

"No thanks. I know the routines pretty well. That's not the problem." Heather lifted her eyes to look at Katie. "I just found out that my grandpa was rushed to the hospital, and I want to get over there. But I've worked so hard for the tryouts. I've always wanted to be a cheerleader. And can you believe it? I'm number 27 out of 29 girls trying out!" Heather's glance dropped. "I don't know if I can wait that long."

Katie's stomach knotted, and her mouth felt

like it was full of cotton. She cared about Heather and knew how awful she must feel. But if she traded her number, she might ruin her chances at making the cheerleading squad. *Well*, she thought, *if I make it, I make it. If I don't, I don't. I guess Heather's grandfather is more important than wanting to perform early on.*

"Listen, Heather, I drew number two. Why don't we trade numbers—then you can get over to the hospital and be with your grandpa."

"Really?" Heather's eyes filled with hope.

"Yeah, really." Katie smiled.

"Number two," the squad director shouted from the other end of the gym. Katie handed her number to Heather, who, after giving Katie a quick hug, darted toward the tryout room. Just to see Heather so excited was worth the trade-off to Katie.

Katie waited another 40 minutes before her number was called. Because she and her sister had spent hours practicing, Katie was just as confident as if she'd been the second to perform. Both she *and* Heather ended up making the squad.

Katie was considerate of her friend's feelings. Being aware of others' emotions and needs are true inner-beauty qualities. Some people are too wrapped up in their own lives to even notice that someone else is hurting.

Considerate people go beyond noticing. They do something about it! They help when it's needed, hug when it comforts, and often do the little jobs no one else wants to do.

Considerate people are not selfish. They strive to put others before themselves. They're kind, loving, and willing to get involved in others' lives. Being considerate is a quality that enhances relationships and develops inner beauty.

Contentment

Do you know people who are peaceful and calming to be around? People who don't complain or get upset, no matter what life throws at them? The apostle Paul was such a person. Writing to the Philippians from his prison cell, Paul said he had learned to be satisfied in all circumstances, in poverty and in prosperity (Philippians 4:11–12). He had learned the secret of being content. Contentment is a characteristic that's found in inwardly attractive people. Being content—or satisfied—means being pleased with, and thankful for, who you are and what you have. This enables you to gracefully accept life's ups and downs and helps you want to make the best out of every situation.

When you're content, you have a true sense of joy and peace deep inside. Smiles come easily. Encouraging others seems natural. Loving life is your way of living.

Being happy with yourself lets you focus your attention on others rather than worrying about yourself.

Contented people help us concentrate on the things that matter—especially the Lord.

Consistency

Jamie found out the hard way that consistency was one of those words with a heavy-duty meaning. She used to shop and go for ice cream with Allison all the time. But when Megan—an upperclassman—began paying attention to her, she began to ignore Allison.

Jamie felt important when she was with Megan. Boys were always around, she heard the latest gossip, and older kids were even learning her name.

So, recently, she'd been making excuses when Allison asked her to come over or go with her to the mall. Instead of being honest with Allison and explaining that she was branching out and making new friends, Jamie lied and said, "I don't feel well," or "I haven't finished my homework yet."

Allison continued to pass Jamie fun little notes between classes and call her on the phone. "Are you sure you're okay?" she'd asked. "I really miss not hanging out with you. Have I done something to hurt your feelings?"

Jamie denied everything and simply said, "I just don't have time anymore to get ice cream. I have more important things to do!"

Allison eventually found other friends and gave up trying to plan things with Jamie. She continued to smile and be friendly whenever she saw Jamie in the hallway, but she quit calling.

Then, just as fast as Megan had noticed Jamie, Megan turned away and started spending time with other friends. When Jamie called Megan or tried to talk with her at school, she received a cold response. "I don't have time for underclassmen," Megan would tell her. "Go find someone your own age to hang out with."

Jamie was devastated. She felt lonely without Megan, and she now felt guilty for excluding Allison. She began to realize what real friendship was all about. Jamie took out a piece of stationery and wrote an apology to Allison.

"I'm really sorry I snubbed you," she wrote. "I was a lousy friend. Can you ever forgive me? I miss you."

The next day at lunch, Allison plopped her lunch tray next to Jamie's. "Care if I sit here?" she asked.

"No," Jamie said. "I'd *love* to have lunch with you!"

Allison and four other girls sat with Jamie and giggled their way through lunch.

That night in her diary, Jamie wrote: "I really lost out for a while. Even though I valued Allison's friendship, I wasn't committed enough to be there when she called. I was an inconsistent friend.

"But Allison is genuine. And stable. That's a *true* friend—one who's dependable and consistent."

Consistency may be the hardest to develop of the three inner-beauty qualities, because we often don't feel like following through on what we say we'll do. But the "yo-yo" person—the person who says one thing and does another—will have a hard time building trust and respect in friendships.

We should follow Jesus' example. He is the model of consistency. He isn't loving one minute and mean the next. He doesn't act like a friend to your face and then say nasty things about you behind your back. He doesn't act concerned with your troubles and then not care. He's consistent. That's one reason we can trust Him.

So, remember: People who are consistent are friends you can count on. They are people who are confident in being themselves—no masks, no games.

WE'RE ALL UNDER CONSTRUCTION

When I (Andrea) first began working on developing my inner beauty, I often asked, "Why do I always feel as though I'm under construction? Will I ever really be beautiful on the inside?" When I grew in one area, the Lord shone His spotlight on another, and the inner-beauty construction process began all over again. I finally realized that growth is a journey. We are *continuously* under construction. With the help of the Holy Spirit, we make ourselves more beautiful by building from the inside outward. We must first decide that we want to develop our inner qualities, and then we must practice, practice, practice. But the result is worth it, because people who are filled with beauty on the inside radiate beauty on the outside, no matter what they look like physically.

Never give up during the construction process. There will be lots of times you'll want to throw in the towel—but don't. Holly didn't. Hanging in there sure paid off for *her*.

Developing Inner Beauty Is A Decision

Holly heard about Jesus at a Christian camp and soon became a believer. The decision to follow Christ seemed easy at the time, but later she found it tough to be 16 and to live for Jesus. She felt so discouraged that she just wanted to quit. "Why does it matter what I act like and what I do?" she wanted to know.

Holly's Bible study group met for breakfast before school on Wednesday mornings. They were in the middle of a study on the fruits of the Spirit when Holly started questioning herself. Love, joy, peace, *patience*. That's the one that stumped her—patience. She was having a hard time learning to be patient. Where was patience when she needed it the most? Right now she needed it at home with her mom.

For the past couple of weeks, Holly's mother had really been getting on her nerves. She couldn't figure out why she was always telling her what to do. "Load the dishwasher, unload the dryer, clean your bedroom, dust the living room, finish your homework, baby-sit for the Stewarts so we can go to dinner with them, help your little brother with the trash."

Holly never got the answer she wanted when she questioned her mother. "Because I said so" didn't help Holly understand why.

One night after a major explosion with her mom, Holly ran crying into her room and slammed the door behind her. "Help me, Lord! I need more patience," she pleaded as she threw herself down on her bed. Holly really needed that particular fruit of the Spirit she was learning about. Every time she spouted off to her mom, it made her feel ugly inside.

Holly knew from her Bible study that God wanted her to be patient. As she lay crying on her bed, she could feel the Holy Spirit working inside her. Suddenly, the thoughts that came to her seemed to be just what she needed. She had to work *with* the Lord rather than *against* Him. She needed to *decide* to act patiently with her mom.

Holly thought back to the fight she'd just had with her mother. If only she had chosen to be patient, as the Holy Spirit was prompting her to do, instead of acting angrily, as her feelings were telling her to do, the scene with her mom might have been totally different.

Her sense of discouragement began to lift. As the weeks and months went on, she had plenty of opportunity to try out her theory. What a surprise! It worked. Patience grew in Holly. She didn't feel so ugly on the inside. She felt better about herself and her new way of acting. Holly's patience on the inside was making her prettier on the outside. She was being kinder with those around her, and she even offered to wash the dishes before her mom could ask. Holly could feel the construction under way, for with the Lord's help, she could act patiently.

Two Scripture passages are helping *us* through the inner-beauty construction process. Psalm 138:8 says, "The Lord will perfect that which concerns me" (Amplified). Philippians 1:6 adds, ". . . being confident of this, that he who began a good work in you will carry it on to completion until the day of Christ Jesus" (New International Version).

Isn't that good news? God is doing good work in you and perfecting you. And it never stops! The construction continues as you and the Lord work on building your inner self.

Beholding His Beauty

God's Word is His love letter to us. Reading that letter provides you with an opportunity to spend some special time with Jesus. The more you know about Him, the more time you'll want to spend with Him through Bible reading and prayer. And the more time you spend with Jesus, the more you'll become like Him and the more His beauty will fill you.

Psalm 27:4 makes this point clear: "The one thing I want from God, the thing I seek most of all, is the privilege of meditating in his Temple, living in his presence every day of my life, delighting in his incomparable perfections and glory."

When you spend time in the Lord's presence and think about what His Word says, you, like Jesus, will shine with a beauty that comes from within. This kind of beauty is lasting. Second Corinthians 4:16 tells us that our outer appearance fades with age, but our inner self—our spirit—is made new and younger every day. Inner beauty that comes from spending time with Jesus will last forever!

No amount of makeup, skin care, hairstyling, or clothes can give you the confidence and inner beauty that Jesus can. All of His qualities are available to you because His Spirit came to live inside you when you accepted Jesus into your heart. Developing inner beauty is possible for all of us if we allow the Holy Spirit to play an active part in our lives.

The bottom line? You are incredibly terrific! God loves you dearly. If the Creator of the universe thinks you're so special, maybe it's time *you* started believing it, too!

For Further Thought...

1. Having a low self-image is common but not healthy. Do you know anyone who suffers from this? List some symptoms of a low self-concept.

2. Have you ever wished you could be someone else? Who would you be? Why?

3. Do you ever feel as if you don't quite measure up to most people? Read 2 Corinthians 10:12–13. What do these verses tell you about comparing yourself with others?

4. Why do you think it's hard for people, particularly girls, to believe God loves them just the way He designed them?

5. Describe how you see yourself right now. What do you think has influenced this image?

6. Like Sarah at the beginning of this book, we all draw conclusions about ourselves from other people's comments. Think of a time when someone said something about *you* that you took to heart. How did it affect your self-image?

7. Have you ever tried to be what someone else wanted you to be? What happened?

8. What are the secret dreams of your heart? What or who is stopping you from fulfilling them?

9. Of the three limiters—physical limitations, lack of knowledge, self-doubt—which one hinders you most often?

10. List three not-so-hot experiences you have had. How did your reactions to these situations affect how you felt about yourself?

11. Is there a person you've been holding a grudge against? Ask God to help you forgive the person, heal your hurt, and then help you be loving toward that person again.

12. Can you think of a negative experience in your life that God worked out for good?

13. What unchangeable circumstances in your life have been damaging your self-image? If you accept these circumstances and ask God to help you make the most of them, what changes might you expect?

14. List any physical features you would change if you could. Circle the ones that are unchangeable. Now ask God to help you love every single part of your appearance—just the way He made you.

15. This next one takes courage! Look into a mirror and, one by one, thank God for every part of you. Remember Psalm 139:14: "I praise you because I am fearfully and wonderfully made" (New International Version).

16. We've *all* been rejected at some time because of our appearance, who we are, or where we're from. Open your heart to Jesus and allow Him to heal the hurt you've experienced. Write Him a letter expressing your feelings.

17. List five characteristics that make you one-of-a-kind.

GOING DEEPER . . .

1. In your own words, define *beauty*—both inner and outer.

2. Describe a person you know who has inner beauty. What does she or he act like, look like, and do for others?

3. Isaiah 53:2 says it wasn't Jesus' appearance that attracted people to Him. What did attract people to Him?

4. Read Proverbs 4:23. The contents of our hearts will determine our actions. So, why is it important for us to watch over our hearts?

5. Are you considerate of the feelings and needs of those closest to you? List the names of your family members. Next to their names jot down what you think their needs are. How can you help fulfill those needs?

6. Being content means being pleased with, and thankful for, who you are and what you have. Contentment leads to peace and joy. Write a paragraph explaining why you *are* or *are not* content.

7. Define *consistency*. Write a brief description of a friend who is consistent and another who is inconsistent. Which one can you count on? Which are *you*?

8. We're all under the inner-beauty construction process. How is the Holy Spirit working to build inner beauty into *your* life?

Hopefully, you've learned some valuable truths about yourself by reading this book. Why not pass around the good stuff? If you have friends who are struggling with low self-esteem, encourage them with what you've learned. And if they're interested, loan them this book!

BRIO

Designed especially for **teen girls**, **Brio** magazine is packed with **super stories**, intriguing interviews and **amusing articles** on the topics girls care about most—**relationships, fitness, fashion** and more—all from a *Christian* perspective.

To request Brio, call Focus on the Family at (719) 531-5181, or write to us at Focus on the Family, Colorado Springs, CO 80995.

New! From your friends at Brio magazine!

The "Let's Talk About Life" Series

Are you curious? Concerned? Have tons of questions? We've put answers to some of your most-asked-about subjects into our new collection of minibooks. Written with you in mind, each is short, easy to read and packed with stuff (insight, info, advice) you'll find *really* helpful.

What You've Always Wanted to Know About Your "."
Though you've probably heard all about it (you may have even started!), chances are you *still* have a bunch of questions about your monthly menstrual cycle. This little book has all the answers, from figuring out what kind of sanitary protection is right for you—and how to use it—to cramps, mood swings and playing sports while menstruating. (And yes, it even tells you where that ridiculous word came from!)

When Someone You Know Is Sexually Abused
Some secrets are tough to keep to oneself. So it's important to know how to respond when a friend confides that she's been mistreated sexually. This book will help you know what to say, when to listen and how to be tender, sensitive and compassionate. It also provides guidelines for whom you should turn to for help and how you can support your friend as she recovers from this ordeal.

are produced by Focus on the Family Publishing.
Distributed in the U.S.A. and Canada by Word Books.
Available at Christian bookstores everywhere.